Humble Heron and Friends

Short Stories, Fuzzy Animals, and Life Lessons

Norma MacDonald

Humble Heron and Friends
Short Stories, Fuzzy Animals, and Life Lessons
Copyright ✻ 2016 Norma MacDonald

Published by: Find Your Way Publishing, Inc.
PO BOX 667
Norway, ME 04268 U.S.A.

www.findyourwaypublishing.com

ISBN-13: 978-0-9849322-6-9
ISBN-10: 0-9849322-6-7

First Edition

Library of Congress Control Number: 2016936238

Dedication

This book is dedicated to all of the people trying to make the world a better place. You are making a positive difference!

"I alone cannot change the world, but I can cast a stone across the waters to create many ripples." ~ Mother Teresa

Table of Contents

About This Book

Welcome to our Karma for Kids Book Series. We are very grateful that you picked up this book. We believe together we can make a positive difference, one child at a time. We strive to instill important life lessons in the lives of young children. We are firm believers in Karma and think that if this simple Law of the Universe is taught to children at a young age, their lives will have the potential to be absolutely amazing.

We once knew a dog named Karma. She was a beautiful, yellow Labrador retriever. It wasn't until after she passed, at 11 years old (God bless her loyal soul.), that we realized just how fitting her name really was.

Karma is indeed a retriever.

Whatever we threw out, Karma was always happy to bring it back to us. It didn't matter what it was, she always brought it back. If we threw out garbage, she'd bring it back without question. If we threw out the most beautiful dog toy, she'd bring it back. It's the same in life. Whatever you send out, is what you will get back. Guaranteed. Every time. Our Karma for Kids Book Series hopes to instill this easy-to-understand Law of the Universe into the lives of children at a young age. The Universe wants to happily bring you all that your heart desires, and it will, effortlessly. But first you've got to throw out what you want it to bring back to you so that it can! Have fun with this and watch the magic happen. God bless!

Find all of Norma MacDonald's Karma for Kids Books at Amazon.com.

For more of our Karma for Kids books please visit us at:

www.karmaforkidsbooks.wordpress.com

Other books that we recommend to help children learn important life lessons:

Billy Brown Bear and Friends: Short Stories, Fuzzy Animals, and Life Lessons By Norma MacDonald

Guaranteed Success for Kindergarten; 50 Easy Things You Can Do Today! By Marrae Kimball

Guaranteed Success for Grade School; 50 Easy Things You Can Do Today! By Marrae Kimball

The Secret Combination to Middle School: Real Advice from Real Kids, Ideas for Success, and Much More! By Marrae Kimball

Thank you!

Humble Heron and Friends

Short Stories, Fuzzy Animals, and Life Lessons

Norma MacDonald

Chapter One

The Festival of Colored Leaves is Cancelled

Humble Heron flapped his big, blue wings as fast as he could. He knew he shouldn't have flown so far away from Fala Forest on Gathering Day. Especially not the day before the festival. But he really, really wanted to see the sparkly white beach his good friend, Jolly Blue Jay, told him about. He was happy he went. The sand sparkled like diamonds and the waves crashed to the shore with loads of bubbly bubbles. Humble Heron made many new friends with the Silly Seagulls. But now he needed to hurry home. He didn't want his family to worry.

As he flew toward home, the sun began to fall behind the giant mountain. The sky changed from blue to orange and the air blew cool against his long bill. Humble Heron needed to hurry. His wings began to tire out. But he didn't want to be late. So he beat them faster, again and again and again.

Just when he thought he could go no further, the edge of the forest appeared below. As he flew closer to the ground, the nests of Hard Worker Woodpecker and Compassionate Cardinal came in sight. Just ahead, Loyal Labrador, Kind

Kittykins, and Playful Puppy walked along the road from the village. Everyone would be at the meeting tonight to get the details about the festival. Humble Heron shivered with excitement. What surprises did the Devoted Deer have to share with them?

Humble Heron's stomach rumbled. He'd missed supper. His parents knew that he went to the beach and might be home late. He sure hoped they'd left him at least one little fish to eat later.

The cliff stood tall at the edge of the lake. Almost home. Humble Heron tilted his left wing and began to fly down toward the Gathering Circle. His family and most of the animals of Fala Forest had already arrived. Perched on the huge, egg-shaped rock, his parents and his little brother and sister waited. They watched the sky for him.

Humble Heron lifted his wings and landed gently beside his father. "Hello, Papa."

His father gave him a stern look. "You almost didn't make it on time, Son. Your mother and I were worried."

Humble Heron told them he was sorry. He didn't want his parents to worry. His mother smiled and nodded. "We're happy you made it home safely. Now rest. The meeting will begin soon."

Cheerful voices filled the air. The animals of Fala Forest and the nearby village buzzed with excitement about the festival. Humble Heron waved to his friends Jolly Blue Jay, Faithful Fox, and Grateful Groundhog. Believer Beaver thumped his tail in greeting. It seemed that everyone had arrived, even Stubborn Squirrel, Selfish Rat, Meany Mouse, Wily Weasel and Rudy Rude Badger. Humble Heron lifted his wing, greeting them all.

The chattering crowd grew quiet as the Devoted Deer stepped into the middle of the circle. Love was the most beautiful deer of all. Wisdom had the brightest eyes. Justice was the tallest. And Power was the strongest. The four deer nodded and dipped their heads to the forest family and village visitors. All the animals sang a welcome song together in many different voices. Some chirped, others squeaked, and the small birds tweet, tweet, tweeted. The forest echoed with the sound of the happy chorus.

When the song finished, the Devoted Deer stomped their hooves to applaud. Birds flapped their wings and Believer Beaver thumped his tail. Wisdom stepped forward and the crowd quieted. "Precious friends, tonight we hoped to talk about the plans for tomorrow's Festival of Colored Leaves, but sadly we have to discuss a serious problem."

Wisdom stepped back and Justice moved forward. "The door to the winter storehouse was left open and some of the food got wet from yesterday's heavy rain. Half of it is ruined."

The animal crowd gasped and shook their heads. No one could believe it. They'd worked very hard for months to fill up that storehouse. Who left the door open? The animals looked around at each other. Rudy Rude Badger pointed at Wily Weasel. "You always leave the door open."

Wily Weasel shouted back. "It wasn't me!"

"Quiet, please!" Love raised a hoof and pawed at the air. "There's no need to blame anyone, my dear ones. Whoever left the door open did it by mistake. The important thing is that we now work together to solve the problem.

Power spoke up in a loud voice. "To survive the cold months, we know we must put away plenty of extra food. The time left is short, so we must take special action."

Humble Heron glanced around the circle of forest friends. Many whispered and nodded in agreement. The Devoted Deer waited for the crowd to quiet down again. Power continued. "Friends, we have decided tomorrow will be an official Food Gathering Day. All of us must help fill the winter storehouse. I'm sorry, but The Festival of Colored Leaves will have to be postponed."

"Oh no!" Many cried. The animals' heads dropped in discouragement. The festival was the happiest day of the year. And everyone knew that winter was very close and there wasn't much food left to be found. How would they do it?

Wisdom acknowledged their concerns. "We're very sorry, but we have no choice. We must all come together tomorrow as soon as the sun lights the sky."

Selfish Rat squeaked at the top of his voice, "But I have to repair my walls tomorrow. I don't have time to help gather food."

Wily Weasel nodded in agreement. "I'm too busy, too."

Many of the other animals also made excuses.

Love, Justice, Wisdom and Power tapped their hooves on the ground to get everyone's attention. "If we all work together, we can fill the storehouse and still have time to do our chores and still have some fun, too. Now let's all go home and get a good night of rest. We'll meet back here at sunrise." Love lifted her hoof and smiled. "Goodnight everyone!"

Humble Heron and his family and all the other friends of Fala Forest went home to their nests, dens, caves, and hollow log homes. Their hearts felt heavy with sadness because the festival was cancelled. Darkness fell over the forest and most of the animals fell right to sleep. Crickets chirped. A big yellow moon rose above the giant mountain making the forest glow in the soft night light.

At sunrise, all the animals rubbed their eyes and yawned as they walked slowly to the Gathering Circle. The Devoted Deer organized everyone with partners and sent each pair in different directions with baskets in hand. Justice stood on a high rock and spoke in a loud voice. "If we can all return with our baskets full before the sun is at the top of the sky, we have arranged a super special surprise for everyone."

The sleepy animals perked up. Hard Worker Woodpecker grabbed his basket and shouted. "Let's get to work!"

The animals searched carefully throughout Fala Forest--left and right, up and down, over and under. They couldn't believe how much food they found. Within a few hours their baskets overflowed with acorns and mushrooms and seeds. The Devoted Deer patted each pair of animals as they brought their baskets to the winter storehouse. After they were emptied, the winter storehouse overflowed with food. Mysteriously, Power and Justice pranced off into the deep forest. Wisdom and Love stayed and congratulated the forest friends. "See what wonderful things we can do when we all work together?"

Faithful Fox stepped to the front of the crowd. "Working together was fun. But what's our special treat?" Animal voices echoed the same question. What could it be?

A few minutes later, Power and Justice appeared from behind the old oak tree carrying a couple of very large baskets. The youngest of the animals bounced up and down all asking the same question. What is it?

All the animals gathered around to peer into the baskets and then together, shouted with glee. "Elderberries!" The juicy purple berries were a favorite treat for the animals of Fala Forest and there was plenty for everyone.

That evening as the sun set on Fala Forest, the animals went home with full bellies and shiny faces. Working together, they had gathered more than enough food to last through the long, cold winter.

Chapter Two

The Missing Hat

Before the first big storm arrived, Humble Heron and his family packed up and headed to a warmer place for the winter, because they didn't like snow. Most of the Fala Forest birds did the same thing. The animals who stayed behind spent most of their days and nights cuddled up together in their warm underground homes. But sometimes the young ones would get tired of being inside all the time, so they'd go out to play.

It had snowed for three days in a row when Faithful Fox peaked her nose out of the family den. Everything glowed white except for the clear blue sky above and the cheerful sun that rose above the trees. She put on her new bright blue scarf, hat, and gloves. They were special gifts from her grandma. The fresh snow glowed so bright, she squinted her eyes as she stepped into the sunlight.

Before long, Reliable Rabbit and Stubborn Squirrel came outside and joined her. They chased each other through the snow, along the edge of the frozen lake, and around and around the great oak tree. Out of breath, they plopped down under the tree for a little rest. Faithful Fox's ears felt cold.

"Oh no!" she cried as she reached up and touched her bare head. "I've lost my hat."

The three friends traced their tracks in the snow back to the frozen lake, but they couldn't find the bright blue hat of Faithful Fox anywhere. Along the way, they stopped and asked several other animals, but no one had seen her hat.

They had almost given up hope of ever finding the hat when they met Loyal Labrador coming into the forest from the village. "I do believe I passed Wily Weasel wearing a blue hat on the path from the village a little while ago."

"Wonderful," said Faithful Fox. "Thank you for your help."

Later that day, Faithful Fox saw Wily Weasel digging holes in the snow near the big oak tree. But he wasn't wearing her hat. She approached him with a warm greeting and then asked about her hat.

Wily weasel continued to dig without looking up at her. "I don't know anything about your hat."

Faithful Fox was surprised. "Oh. I'm sorry. Loyal Labrador thought he saw you wearing it earlier today. He must have been mistaken."

"Must have been," Wily Weasel muttered.

Faithful Fox continued searching for her bright blue hat. As she passed by the rabbit warren, Reliable Rabbit popped her head out of the hole. "Did you get your hat back from Wily Weasel?"

"Wily Weasel doesn't have it."

Reliable Rabbit gave Faithful Fox a funny look. "Of course he does. I saw him wearing it when he passed by here half an hour ago."

"Are you sure it was my bright blue hat?"

"Sure as sure can be," said Reliable Rabbit.

Faithful Fox felt sad and frustrated. Reliable Rabbit always told the truth. Why had Wily Weasel lied about her hat? What could she do about it? She decided the best thing to do would be to go home and ask her parents.

When she got back to her family den, her parents could see right away that something was wrong. She told them about losing her hat and what Loyal Labrador and Reliable Rabbit said about seeing Wily Weasel wearing it. "But Wily Weasel said he didn't know anything about my hat. I think he might be lying. What should I do?"

"We're so sorry to hear this. We know that hat is very special to you because your grandmother made it," said Mama Fox.

Her father sat up. "Do you think it's possible that one of the other weasels was wearing the hat and Loyal Labrador and Reliable Rabbit thought it was Wily Weasel?"

Faithful Fox thought for a minute. "I guess that's possible."

"How about the three of us go visit the Weasel family's den and see what we can find out."

When they arrived, Papa Weasel invited them in. After Faithful Fox's parents explained what happened, Papa Weasel called Wily Weasel into the room. "Son, is it really true you haven't seen Faithful Fox's bright blue hat today?"

Wily Weasel glanced around the room, eyes shifting back and forth. He didn't look anyone in the face. "I already told her I haven't seen it."

One of the youngest of the Weasel Family entered the den. "What's this about a blue hat?"

"Faithful Fox lost her blue hat today, have you seen it?" asked Mama Weasel.

The little weasel disappeared into the one of the small rooms and came back carrying Faithful Fox's hat. "Is this the one?"

Faithful Fox gave a big smile and clapped. "My hat! Where did you find it?"

"In Wily Weasel's bedroom. He came home wearing it earlier today."

Everyone turned and stared at Wily Weasel. He turned bright red. "But I found it on the ground close to the lake. Finders keepers, losers weepers."

Both sets of parents shook their heads. Papa Weasel apologized to the Fox Family. "Please forgive our son. It seems he still has quite a few lessons to learn. Please know that we will have a long talk about telling the truth after you leave. But for now, Wily Weasel, you need to apologize. What you did was wrong."

"I'm sorry." Wily Weasel said, as he lowered his head in shame.

Faithful Fox walked up to him and patted his shoulder. "I forgive you for lying about my hat. If you'd like, maybe I can ask my grandma to make one for you, too."

Wily Weasel perked up a little bit. "Really? Thanks."

Faithful Fox took her hat and with her parents, walked home through the crunchy snow toward their cozy den. On the way, Papa Fox talked about how important it is to tell the truth. "When someone lies, everyone gets hurt."

"True," said Mama Fox. "And it makes it very hard to trust each other."

Faithful Fox pulled her hat down over her ears. "I sure hope Wily Weasel will stop lying from now on."

Mama Fox wrapped her arm around her daughter. "Yes, dear. And I think you need to be more careful not to lose your things."

Faithful Fox hugged her Mama. "I promise I will try not to lose anything again. Especially not my special hat."

Chapter Three

What Happened to Believer Beaver's Dam?

The spring rains arrived early in Fala Forest and melted all the snow. White flowers pushed their way through the forest floor along with many other bright green plants. The giant oak tree began to show signs of blooms and leaves. Many of the bird families returned to the forest and were busy building new nests.

The Heron family was the last to come home to Fala Forest. Humble Heron was eager to catch up with all his friends and share with them the adventures he'd had at his family's warm winter home on the shores of the wide river. He also wanted to hear all about how the winter turned out for those who stayed in Fala Forest.

Jolly Blue Jay was the first friend to come by and greet him. "I'm so happy to see you. I thought you might never come back!"

Humble Heron laughed. "You know we're always the last ones home. It's a long trip and Mama and Papa like to stop and catch fish at every big lake we pass along the way."

"Well, "said Jolly Blue Jay, "You are just in time for the first spring picnic. Grateful

Groundhog invited everyone to go to Morning Glory Meadow tomorrow afternoon to eat and play games. Can you come?"

"I think I can. I will go ask my parents."

That night the wind blew in a huge storm. Thunder crashed, lightning flashed and the rain came down like a waterfall. Many of the Fala Forest animals had to come above ground as the water flooded into their homes. But by morning, the rain had stopped and the sun began to dry everything out. Many animals went to the Gathering Circle to find out if everyone was okay. The Devoted Deer made an announcement that most of the families had survived the storm without any trouble and that those whose homes were damaged were getting the help they needed.

The young ones could go ahead with their picnic in Morning Glory Meadow.

When the sun was at the top of the sky, Grateful Groundhog waited for everyone to meet under the giant oak tree. Most of the young forest friends had arrived, including Loyal Labrador, Kind Kittykins and Playful Puppy who had come all the way from the village. The air buzzed with excitement. Picnics in Morning Glory Meadow were so fun!

Compassionate Cardinal flew around to make sure everyone had arrived before they left for the meadow. But someone was missing. "Has anyone seen Believer Beaver?"

Everyone shook their heads "no".

Grateful Groundhog stood on a log and pointed toward the meadow. "We will pass by the Beaver Family dam on the way to the meadow. Maybe Believer Beaver is waiting for us there."

The group of animals followed each other along the narrow path around the shore to where the water flowed from the lake where the Beaver Family had built their dam.

But the dam was gone!

Everyone was so surprised. What happened to it? Humble Heron flapped his wings and pointed across the creek. "There he is!" He waved to Believer Beaver and called out. "Come on over. We're on our way to Morning Glory Meadow for a picnic. You're still coming, right?"

Believer Beaver slowly crossed the creek and came out of the water with eyes filled with tears. "I wish I could, but the rain swept away our dam and flooded our lodge last night. We have so much work to do to build another. I've been working since early this morning and my teeth are so tired from cutting down so many trees."

Many of the animals surrounded Believer Beaver and took turns giving hugs. "We're so sorry about your house," they said.

"Where are your parents?" asked Grateful Groundhog.

"They went deep into the woods with a group of helpers to find bigger trees," said Believer Beaver.

Grateful Groundhog sighed in relief. "I'm so glad to hear everyone is okay."

Selfish Rat shifted from one foot to the other with impatience. "Yes. We're sorry and all that, but we can't cut down trees for you. And we've got a picnic waiting for us in the meadow. So see ya later. Let's get moving everyone."

Compassionate Cardinal flew to the top of a nearby tree. "There must be something we can do to help Believer Beaver."

Selfish Rat shook his head. "The Devoted Deer said they were indeed being helped and Believer Beaver just said a group went with his parents. There's nothing we can do. Now let's go."

"But the Devoted Deer have taught us that we need to be kind. And kindness means helping each other through hard times. Just like when we all worked together to fill the storehouse. I think we should stay and find a way to help."

Half of the animals followed Selfish Rat, the other half stayed behind with Compassionate Cardinal and talked about what they could do to help the Beaver Family rebuild their dam.

Believer Beaver thanked them all. "Besides cutting down small trees, I need to gather many small tree limbs and sticks. Maybe some of you could do that for me."

Grateful Groundhog, Humble Heron, Compassionate Cardinal and the friends from the village spent the rest of the day helping the Beaver Family rebuild their home. The birds carried small sticks in their beaks and Loyal Labrador, Kind

Kittykins and Playful Puppy carried small tree limbs in their mouths.

Half way through the afternoon, a couple of the animals who followed Selfish Rat to Morning Glory Meadow returned, including Rudy Rude Badger who wasn't known for being kind. Stubborn Squirrel explained. "We just couldn't stop thinking about how mean it was to go eat and play while the rest of you stayed and worked so hard."

At the end of the day, the Devoted Deer stopped by with a feast for everyone to share. "We wanted to reward all of you for the beautiful kindness you showed to the Beaver Family."

As they were finishing up the delicious meal of nuts and berries and fresh grass, Selfish Rat and the few others who spent the whole day at Morning Glory Meadow returned. "What's this?" Selfish Rat asked. "Why did you plan a special dinner and not invite us?"

Rudy Rude Badger spoke up quickly. "This feast is a reward for our kindness. You didn't help. So go away."

Compassionate Cardinal shook his head at Rudy Rude Badger. "Now that's not the way to show kindness. We've all had plenty to eat. The kind thing for us to do now is share what's left." He gestured to Selfish Rat. "Help yourselves."

As Selfish Rat helped himself to the special dinner, he felt in his heart that he had done the wrong thing. He could feel it. He just knew. "I'm sorry that I didn't help. I promise to do better next time."

The Devoted Deer watched from a distance and nodded their heads in approval.

That night the Beaver Family slept safely in their new lodge. And all the Fala Forest friends went to bed feeling the happy effects of kindness.

Norma MacDonald

Chapter Four

The Freeze Dance Game

The air outside warmed as summer drew ever closer. Many of the Fala Forest trees blossomed pink and yellow and white. The young animals had lots of time to fly or swim or play games together. There was much food to be found everywhere. No one had to worry. All the animals seemed relaxed and happy.

One beautiful, sunny afternoon, Jolly Blue Jay collected all the young animals together in the Wild Cherry Grove. The trees were covered with pink blossoms that would someday become yummy red cherries. When the wind blew, the flowers whirled around like confetti before falling lightly to the ground. It was the perfect place for a game of Freeze Dance.

All the young animals of Fala Forest loved to play Freeze Dance. The Musical Magpies would sing a fun song and everyone would dance. In the middle of the song, the birds would stop singing and all the dancing animals would have to freeze in the middle of their dance move. One of the animals would be made the Dance Freeze Judge and would watch to see if anyone moved. If one moved, one had to spend the rest of the game skipping through the wild cherry trees until someone became the Freeze Dance Champion.

The Musical Magpies perched high in the tallest cherry tree waiting for Jolly Blue Jay to choose who would be the Freeze Dance Judge for the day. Many of the animals raised their tails to be judge, but Jolly Blue Jay chose Meany Mouse because she'd never had a chance to be the judge before. Some of the animals groaned. They didn't want Meany Mouse to be the judge. But Jolly Blue Jay wanted to be fair and make sure all the animals got a chance at the job.

Some of the animals practiced their favorite dance moves while the Musical Magpies were warming up their voices. Faithful Fox and Wily Weasel were really great dancers and everyone cheered as they showed their latest dance steps.

When it was time for the music to start, everyone found a place in the middle of the Wild Cherry Grove. The ground was covered with blossoms. Each time someone moved their feet, tiny pink flower petals flew up into the sweet-smelling air.

The Musical Magpies began to twitter their first song and all the young animals twirled and whirled around. When the music stopped, they all tried to freeze in place. Some of the birds had to hold their wings high in the air, other animals had to stand on one foot, while others had to keep their tails pointed out straight. Meany Mouse walked through the frozen-in-place animals with her whiskers twitching, eager to catch someone moving.

Wily Weasel froze in a super hard position — both arms in the air and standing on one foot. As

Meany Mouse walked by, her tail brushed Wily Weasel's ankle. It tickled so much, he just couldn't stand still. When he moved, Meany Mouse pointed, "You're out."

"That's not fair!" Wily Weasel argued. "You tickled me with your tail."

"I did not," she said. "Now stop making excuses and get skipping."

"Not fair," Wily Weasel grumbled as he walked over to the nearest cherry tree and began to skip around the cherry trees.

The music started again and all the forest animals began to dance. Some of them danced with each other and some danced alone. The music stopped and everyone froze. Faithful Fox fell over in a fit of giggles. Meany Mouse pointed to the cherry trees and so Faithful Fox skipped over and joined Wily Weasel.

Meany Mouse slid in and out between the rest of the frozen dancers, tail whipping back and forth. Believer Beaver cried out as she walked by. "Watch that tail. You just hit me in the face!"

Meany Mouse scowled. "Your mouth moved, which means you're out. To the trees with you!"

"What?" cried Believer Beaver. "That's not fair."

True, it wasn't fair. But the judge was the one to decide and she was right, Believer Beaver's mouth did move. What the animals didn't know was that the Devoted Deer watched them from a distance.

The Musical Magpies continued their beautiful music and the remaining animals danced and danced. When the music stopped this time, Rudy Rude Badger and Hard Worker Woodpecker froze and then fell over. Meany Mouse pointed them to the cherry trees.

That meant only five animals were still in the game—Humble Heron, Jolly Blue Jay, Grateful Groundhog, Compassionate Cardinal, and Stubborn Squirrel. All of them stayed frozen in their positions. They tried hard not to even blink an eye as Meany Mouse passed close by.

A bee buzzed around Grateful Groundhog's nose. He couldn't help himself. He had to swat it away. Meany Mouse sent him out. Then she circled around the three birds and Stubborn Squirrel. No one moved. The wind blew a cherry blossom into Stubborn Squirrel's eye and she couldn't help but brush it away.

"You're outta here," said Meany Mouse.

"But that wasn't my fault," cried Stubborn Squirrel. "If it weren't for the blossom, I wouldn't have moved."

Meany Mouse folded her arms across her chest. "You moved. You're out. No argument."

The Musical Magpies started up a new tune and the three birds hopped and bounced and twirled and whirled. All the rest of the animals who had gone out watched while they skipped around the cherry trees. Before long, the music stopped, the birds froze, and Meany Mouse scurried over to each animal. Again her little tail brushed against their legs. Everyone could tell she was doing it on purpose in order to tickle them. She didn't need to get so close to them.

Jolly Blue Jay couldn't stand it anymore. "Stop that tickling!" he shouted. "How are we supposed to stand still with that little tail of yours bothering us?"

Humble Heron and Compassionate Cardinal nodded in agreement. "None of us can keep frozen with that tickly little tail touching us."

Meany Mouse waved her arms. "You all moved so you're all out! That means I'm the winner since none of you were able to stay frozen."

The three birds and the rest of the animals circled around Meany Mouse. "Not fair. You cheated. You made us move on purpose with that tail of yours."

Meany Mouse shook her head. "I did not cheat. You all moved so you all lost the game."

As the young animals argued, the Devoted Deer approached quietly from behind. Wisdom stepped into the young animal circle and everyone stopped talking. "We've been watching you play on this beautiful afternoon, but it appears things have turned ugly. What seems to be the problem?"

Wily Weasel, who was the first animal Meany Mouse kicked out after tickling him with her tail, explained. "She cheated. She used her tail to get us to move when we were frozen." He pointed in her face. "Cheater. Cheater. Cheater."

Justice stepped up beside Wisdom and questioned Meany Mouse. "Is it true what they say? Did you touch them with your tail?"

Meany Mouse's nose twitched. "Maybe. But I didn't do it on purpose."

"But you don't really need to get so close that your tail touches them, do you?"

"I guess not, "said Meany Mouse.

"Well then, I suggest you start over and this time Meany Mouse will judge without getting so close. We'll be standing by to make sure the game is played fair."

Happy to play another round of Freeze Dance, all the animals cheered. In the end, the game finished with Faithful Fox and Wily Weasel standing still. Neither of them moved. Both were declared the winners. And Meany Mouse discovered that she liked the game better when she played it the right way. It was a lot of fun and not having everyone mad at her was a plus too. The pink blossoms continued to float to the ground and all the young animals of Fala Forest returned home skipping with happiness.

Chapter Five

The Heart Knows

The sun shone brightly and the days grew warmer as spring turned to summer in Fala Forest. Cute little baby foxes, groundhogs, deer, birds, squirrels and many others scampered around the woods. Their mothers and fathers kept busy chasing them around and keeping them from danger.

On one especially hot afternoon, Believer Beaver got the idea to gather all the older young ones for a hike up to the Wondrous Waterfall to play and swim. The animals would be gone all day, so they needed permission from their parents. For most of them that wasn't a problem. Except for Hardworker Woodpecker. His family always had some project to keep them busy.

Hardworker Woodpecker had worked very hard for three days to hollow out a hole for a new nest in the big birch tree at the edge of the lake. He wasn't quite done, but he wanted very much to go to the Wondrous Waterfall and play and splash in the water with the other animals. He approached his parents and asked if he could take the next day off.

"You've done a good job so far with your new nest," said Papa Woodpecker. "But I would like to see you finish before you take time off to play. If you can finish by the end of the day, you can go to the Wondrous Waterfall tomorrow."

"Thank you, Papa," said Hardworker Woodpecker and he worked as fast as he could for the rest of the day, peck, peck, pecking at the hole to make it big enough to live in. Until, he ran into a problem. A super hard stubborn knot slowed down his progress. He tried and tried, but he just couldn't finish by the time the sun fell behind the giant mountain.

As he went to sleep, he thought maybe he could get up super early and finish the nest so that he could still go to the Wondrous Waterfall with his friends. But he slept late. When he opened his eyes the next morning, the sun had already brightened the skies and his friends were knocking at his door. "Ready to go?" asked Jolly Blue Jay.

Hardworker Woodpecker wanted to be obedient to his father, but he also really, really wanted a day off to play with his friends. "Maybe I can go with them for part of the day," he thought. "Then I can come home early and finish the nest."

Without another thought, Hardworker Woodpecker joined the group and started the long hike to the Wondrous Waterfall. The animals scurried up the windy path while the birds flew above them. It took over an hour before they heard the rushing sound of the water falling over the big rocks. Refreshing cool air hit their faces as the animals approached the place where the water from the giant falls tumbled down and collected into a large pool.

"Let's have a swim," shouted Playful Puppy. He jumped into the pool and doggy paddled around in small circles. Believer Beaver joined in, using that big wide beaver tail to slap the water. The rest of the animals joined him. Humble Heron, Jolly Blue Jay, Hardworker Woodpecker, and Compassionate Cardinal splashed around in the shallow part of the pool. They used their wings to splatter each other with cool drops of crystal clear water.

When they'd tired themselves out, they stretched out on the sandy beach to dry out. Then they went to find some nuts and berries to fill their hungry bellies. When they'd eaten as much as their little tummies could hold, they found a cool spot under a large sycamore tree to relax and enjoy the refreshing breeze that gently blew and rustled the leaves. The steady roar of the waterfall made them sleepy, so the animals closed their eyes and took a nap.

When they woke up, the sun had begun to dip behind the giant mountain. Hardworker Woodpecker realized how late it was and panicked. "Oh no! It can't be so close to sunset already. I have to get back and finish my nest!" He took off and flew down the path before any of the animals could ask him why he had to leave in such a rush.

As Hardworker Woodpecker flew towards home, he thought about how angry his father would be when he learned that he'd disobeyed him. He had no excuse for what he'd done.

Saddened in his heart, he decided to go talk to his father and admit his mistake.

Papa Woodpecker was hard at work hollowing out a bigger nest for his newly hatched family. He asked Hardworker Woodpecker if he'd finished his own new nest.

"That's what I came here to talk to you about," said Hardworker Woodpecker, his bright red head lowered in shame. "I haven't finished yet."

"Yes, sometimes it takes a long time to make a big enough hole in these hard wood trees. Keep working at it. I'm sure you'll be done soon," his father said.

"But Papa. I didn't finish because I spent the day playing up at the Wondrous Waterfall with my friends."

His father looked at him with shock. "You disobeyed me?"

Hardworker Woodpecker swallowed in nervousness. "I did. And I came here to apologize and accept whatever punishment you give me. I know I did wrong, and I take full responsibility for it."

Papa Woodpecker let out a long sigh and whistled. "Son, I am sorry to hear you didn't listen to me, but I'm also quite proud of you for coming here and admitting what you did. That shows that you truly do honor your mother and me, despite your disobedience. I'm not going to punish you this time."

"You aren't?" Hardworker Woodpecker was surprised. He didn't think he'd honored his father at all. "But I went and played when I should have been working on my nest."

His father wrapped his wing around him. "You have always worked very hard to help the family. It's good to take some time off and have some fun every once in a while. But I didn't want you to go to the waterfall today because I wanted you to learn that it's important to finish your work before you go off and play. You disobeyed, and did wrong. But you made it right by coming to me and telling me the truth. I'm proud of you, son."

"Thank you, Papa," said Hardworker Woodpecker. "Now I think I'd better go get some rest so I can be sure to finish my new nest first thing in the morning."

Chapter Six

Everyone Plays an Important Role

The young animals in Fala Forest had a splendid summer filled with games and hikes and swimming and tree climbing and all the other fun things forest animals find to do. Most of them wished the summer could go on forever. But like always, the seasons changed. The air began to cool as summer turned into autumn which would soon lead into another cold winter. The leaves on the trees turned from green to yellow, red and orange. The time had come to get busy preparing for another icy winter.

Most of the birds prepared for their long journey south to warmer places. The animals who spent the winter holed up in their little homes had to eat lots and lots of food to fatten up before going into their big sleep. Some of the animals, like the chipmunks, piled loads of nuts in their homes so they could eat them during the winter when they couldn't go outside. Many animals also worked hard to fill the winter storehouse with food, just as they had the year before.

Meany Mouse and Selfish Rat had been working together for several days collecting nuts and berries and seeds. They were tired, so they took a rest in the shade of the big oak tree. Selfish Rat let out a big sigh. "I'm sick and tired of gathering food every day. Why can't our parents take care of gathering food? We're young. We shouldn't have to be doing all of this work."

Meany Mouse agreed. "And the youngest ones don't have to do anything. My little brother and sister have been playing chase every day."

The two animals were soon joined by Stubborn Squirrel. "If I have to gather one more acorn, I think I'll die," he said as he plopped down beside them. "All we ever do anymore is work, work, work."

Compassionate Cardinal listened from a tree branch above their heads. They didn't know he was there. Before long, Rudy Rude Badger walked by. "Why aren't the three of you out collecting food?" he asked.

"Because we're *tired*," said Meany Mouse. "Tired of working all the time. I think we've done enough. Let the older ones finish. It's not like we eat that much anyway."

Wily Weasel came around from the other side of the tree. "Is it break time? I'm exhausted. I can't take another step."

Rudy Rude Badger sat down next to Wily Weasel. "If you're all quitting, I'm stopping, too. Why should I keep working if no one else is?"

Compassionate Cardinal flew down in front of them. "I understand that you're all tired, but think about the coming winter. You don't want to go hungry, do you?"

But the five young animals wouldn't listen. They continued to complain to each other for another hour. Many of the other young animals passed by and heard them grumbling. They shook their heads. Grateful Groundhog listened to their whining for a moment. "Have you thought about what would happen if all the animals in Fala Forest felt the same as you? No one would gather food and everyone would starve this winter. Or, what if there was no food to be gathered? What would we do then?"

But the five grumpy animals didn't listen. They went on grumbling for the rest of the afternoon. Hardworker Woodpecker flew by and noticed the five weren't doing anything. He asked what was wrong. They told him they were tired of working all the time and didn't care what anyone else thought. Hardworker Woodpecker couldn't believe his ears. How could they be so ungrateful? He decided to go talk to the Devoted Deer about what he'd seen and heard.

The Devoted Deer listened patiently to Hardworker Woodpecker. He wasn't the first one to come to them. They'd also heard the same concerns from Compassionate Cardinal and several others. The Devoted Deer decided they needed to have a special meeting at the Gathering Circle. So they asked the Musical Magpies to fly around Fala Forest singing the special song that let everyone know they would have a meeting that evening.

A special meeting got all the animals of Fala Forest excited. Why did the Devoted Deer want them to meet together? They wouldn't have to wait long to find out. After all the animals gathered and sang their happy greeting song, Wisdom and Love took turns explaining the reason for the meeting. "It's been brought to our attention that some of the young animals are having a hard time with the food collection and need some encouragement," said Wisdom.

Love smiled. "So we talked about it and came up with an idea that might help all the animals feel more joyful and motivated."

The animals of Fala Forest whispered to each other. What could it be? What would they do?

Wisdom got everyone's attention and explained. "We have so much to be thankful for here in our peaceful forest, but sometimes we forget. So tonight we're going to remember all the things that make our lives happy. We've decided to give everyone the chance to come into the circle and share at least one thing they're grateful for."

"Let's start with our young ones. Could the young animals please join us here in the middle of the circle?" asked Love.

When all the young animals got to the circle, Wisdom asked Meany Mouse, Selfish Rat, and Stubborn Squirrel to be the first to speak.

"What am I supposed to say?" asked Meany Mouse in a nervous little voice.

"Tell everyone one thing that you are grateful for. Something you are happy about."

Meany Mouse scrunched up her face as she thought about it. All the other young animals did the same. After a minute, Meany Mouse snapped her fingers. "I know. I know. I'm grateful for the delicious seeds that fall from the giant yellow sunny flowers."

Selfish Rat was next. "I'm grateful for apples. Bright red shiny apples are the best."

"Pumpkin seeds," said Stubborn Squirrel. "They're my favorite."

For the next hour, all the animals of Fala Forest got to tell everyone what they were most grateful for. Many of them talked about food, but others talked about how much they appreciated their homes, their friends, their families, and the beautiful forest they lived in with its trees and mountains, lakes and waterfalls.

The Devoted Deer explained that each and every animal played an important role by working together. "You are all very important. You all contribute. We are thankful for all of you." At the end of the evening, when they'd all had a chance to share, the animals went home feeling encouraged, happy and thankful for the many wonderful things they enjoyed in Fala Forest.

Afterword

Thanks again for picking up this book! You are participating in making our world a better place.

For more of our Karma for Kids books please visit us at:

www.karmaforkidsbooks.wordpress.com

Find Norma MacDonald and her books online at Amazon.com.

Other books that we recommend to help children learn important life lessons:

Billy Brown Bear and Friends: Short Stories, Fuzzy Animals, and Life Lessons By Norma MacDonald

Guaranteed Success for Kindergarten; 50 Easy Things You Can Do Today! By Marrae Kimball

Guaranteed Success for Grade School; 50 Easy Things You Can Do Today! By Marrae Kimball

The Secret Combination to Middle School: Real Advice from Real Kids, Ideas for Success, and Much More! By Marrae Kimball

If you have ideas for stories, please feel free to send them to:

Melissa Eshleman

Find Your Way Publishing, Inc.

PO Box 667

Norway, ME 04268

Melissa@findyourwaypublishing.com

Thank you!